Pilchard Goes Fishing

Bob the Builder

Pilchard Goes Fishing

HINKLER BOOKS

One morning, the machines heard some very strange noises coming from the house.

"Oh, you, you be still! Wooah! Heh heh! You're a slippery customer, aren't you?" they heard Bob say from inside.

Just then Wendy arrived. "Morning everyone!" she said. "Where's Bob?"

"He's in the house, Wendy," said Scoop.

"Talking to someone ..." said Muck uncertainly.

3

Inside, Wendy found Bob poking in the fish tank with a net. "Yup, come on," said Bob. Pilchard was watching with great interest.

"Oh. Where you going? … Ah … Oh!" said Bob.

"Bob?" giggled Wendy. "What *are* you doing?"

"Ohh! G'morning, Wendy," said Bob. "I thought it was about time I cleaned out Finn's tank. But he's not helping. Are you Finn?"

"No, I can see that," Wendy laughed. "You get going Bob. I'll take care of Finn."

"Thanks, Wendy," said Bob. "See you later," said Wendy.

Pilchard was still watching Finn closely. "Miaooow!" she said.

In the yard, the machines were ready for work.

"Muck, I'll need you to help me; and Dizzy and Roley," said Bob.

"Can we fix it?" called Scoop.

"YES WE CAN!!!" everyone shouted.

Bob jumped on Muck and they headed out to fix some holes in the road.

"Er, shall I start mixing, Bob?" asked Dizzy when they arrived at the job.

"Yes, Dizzy. You do that … Oh no! I forgot the cement!" cried Bob. "Muck, would you go back to the yard and get a couple of bags for me please?"

"On my way Bob," said Muck.

"And hurry. We've got lots more to do today!" called Bob.

Meanwhile, Wendy put Finn in a bucket of water so she could clean his tank. Suddenly, she heard a loud crash in the yard and rushed outside with the bucket. Muck had come roaring into the yard and swerved to avoid Bird, crashing into the post of the car port.

"Oh," cried Wendy. "Are you all right, Muck?"

"I'm OK. Oh, I'm really sorry, Wendy," said Muck miserably. "Bob sent me back for some cement and he said to hurry and I did but I hurried a bit too fast and … you won't tell him, will you?"

"Oh Muck. Bob'll understand," soothed Wendy.

Wendy put Finn's bucket down and went to inspect the broken post.

"This shouldn't be too hard to fix," said Wendy. "Now, we'll have to dig this out and we'll need to set a new support in cement."

"Cement! That's what I came for!" said Muck.

Wendy put three bags of cement into Muck's tipper. While she was busy, Pilchard snuck over to peek into Finn's bucket.

"See you later, Wendy. And thanks!" called Muck, heading back.

At the site, Dizzy mixed and poured the cement that Muck brought and Roley started rolling it flat.

Bob's cell phone rang. "Hello, Bob the Builder. Oh hi, Wendy," said Bob as he answered it. "Yes, course you can. Bye bye." Bob clipped his phone back on his tool belt. "Dizzy? Could you go back and help Wendy? She needs to have some cement mixed."

"Goody!" cried Dizzy.

"I wonder what Wendy wants cement for?" mused Bob.

Muck groaned, feeling very guilty.

At the yard, Pilchard was still watching Finn closely, while Wendy and Lofty were busy fixing the shelter.

"All right Lofty," said Wendy. "I just want you to pull the old support out of the ground."

"Oh. Er … yeah … I think I can do that," said Lofty, as he began to pull hard on the stump.

"I can lift it … ah … I can lift it!" Lofty muttered, straining.

While Lofty worked, Pilchard took her chance to slide a paw into Finn's bucket.

Suddenly, Lofty freed the stump from the ground with a mighty tug that sent it flying toward Pilchard.

"Miaooow!" squealed Pilchard as she jumped quickly out of the way.

"Ohh, right!" said Wendy. "While we're waiting for Dizzy, I think I'll make some iced tea."

As soon as Wendy went inside, Pilchard crept back over to the bucket.

"Miaow ..." said Pilchard, as she looked in. Just then, Dizzy arrived back in the yard.

"Hi Wendy! I'm home!" shouted Dizzy. Pilchard was surprised and leapt away.

"Oh my! What happened?" said Dizzy when she saw the damaged shelter.

"Oh, just a little accident," said Wendy, coming out of the house. "But now that you're here Dizzy, you can help us. We need some cement in this hole to hold the new support."

"Oh goody!" grinned Dizzy. "I've got lots left." She began to mix.

17

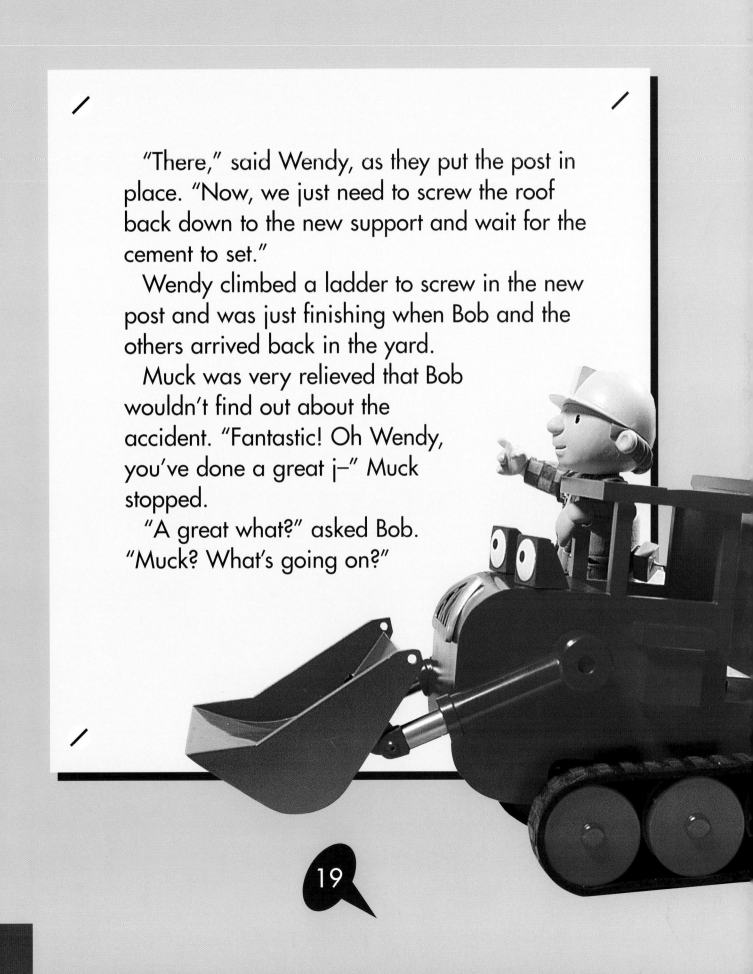

"There," said Wendy, as they put the post in place. "Now, we just need to screw the roof back down to the new support and wait for the cement to set."

Wendy climbed a ladder to screw in the new post and was just finishing when Bob and the others arrived back in the yard.

Muck was very relieved that Bob wouldn't find out about the accident. "Fantastic! Oh Wendy, you've done a great j–" Muck stopped.

"A great what?" asked Bob. "Muck? What's going on?"

"Oh … I had a little accident, Bob," said Muck uneasily. "I skidded to miss Bird and smashed into the car port … Sorry Bob."

"There's no need to be sorry," said Bob.

"You didn't do it on purpose. And Bird's fine."

"Toot, toot, toot!" said Bird in agreement.

"And Wendy, our excellent builder, has fixed it," said Bob.

While they talked, Pilchard crept back to Finn's bucket and licked her lips. This time she was sure she'd catch Finn.

"Toot, toot, TOOT!!" cried Bird, to warn the others.

"Wrrrrooowiaow!!!" said Pilchard angrily.

"Oh Pilchard! Bird!" cried Wendy.
"I totally forgot poor Finn! With all the excitement with the accident and everything, I forgot I was cleaning out the fish tank. But Pilchard and Bird have just reminded me!"

Wendy and Bob went inside to finish the clean-up.

"There you go, Finn. Now your tank's nice and clean, thanks to Wendy," said Bob, as he popped Finn back into his sparkling tank. Pilchard flicked her tail in annoyance. She knew she had missed her chance to go fishing.

"Pilchard?" called Wendy. "You've been such a clever cat, you deserve a special treat, don't you? Would you like some fresh fish?"

But Pilchard had had quite enough fish for one day. "Wrroaww" she sighed, as she collapsed on the floor.

The End

Hinkler Books Pty Ltd 2004
17-23 Redwood Drive
Dingley, VIC 3172 Australia
www.hinklerbooks.com

© 2004 HIT Entertainment PLC and Keith Chapman
All rights reserved. Bob the Builder and all related logos and characters are trademarks
of HIT Entertainment PLC and Keith Chapman.
US edition published in 2002 by Simon Spotlight.

Pilchard Goes Fishing - First published in the UK in 1998 by BBC Worldwide, Ltd.
Based on the script by Jimmy Hibbert.
With thanks to HOT Animation.

ISBN: 1 8651 5983 2
Printed and bound in China